D0341205

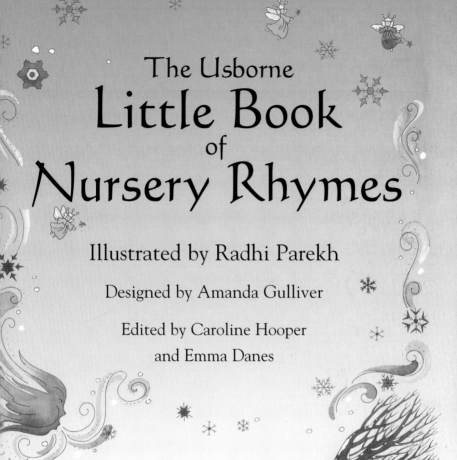

The Usborne
Little Book
of
Nursery Rhymes

Illustrated by Radhi Parekh

Designed by Amanda Gulliver

Edited by Caroline Hooper
and Emma Danes

Contents

Humpty Dumpty

Humpty Dumpty sat on a wall,
Humpty Dumpty had a great fall;
All the King's horses and all the King's men
Couldn't put Humpty together again.

Sing a song of sixpence

Sing a song of sixpence, a pocket full of rye,
Four and twenty blackbirds baked in a pie.
When the pie was opened, the birds began to sing,
Wasn't that a dainty dish to set before the King?

The King was in his counting-house, counting out his money;
The Queen was in the parlor, eating bread and honey;
The maid was in the garden, hanging out the clothes,
When down came a blackbird and pecked off her nose.

If all the world were paper

If all the world were paper,
And all the sea were ink,
And all the trees were bread and cheese,
What should we have to drink?

Rub-a-dub-dub

Rub-a-dub-dub,
Three men in a tub,
And who do you think they be?
The butcher, the baker,
The candlestick-maker,
So turn out the knaves, all three.

Old King Cole

Old King Cole
Was a merry old soul,
And a merry old soul was he;
He called for his pipe,
And he called for his bowl,
And he called for his fiddlers three.

Every fiddler, he had a fiddle,
And a very fine fiddle had he;
Oh, there's none so rare
As can compare
With King Cole and his fiddlers three.

Jack Sprat

Jack Sprat could eat no fat,
His wife could eat no lean,
And so between them both, you see,
They licked the platter clean.

Mary had a little lamb

Mary had a little lamb,
Its fleece was white as snow,
And everywhere that Mary went,
The lamb was sure to go.

It followed her to school one day,
That was against the rule;
It made the children laugh and play,
To see a lamb at school.

And so the teacher turned it out,
   But still it lingered near;
And waited for her patiently,
   Till Mary did appear.

"Why does the lamb love Mary so?"
   The children all did cry;
"Why, Mary loves the lamb, you know,"
   The teacher did reply.

Three blind mice

Three blind mice, three blind mice,
See how they run! See how they run!
They all ran after the farmer's wife
Who cut off their tails with a butcher's knife;
Did you ever see such a thing in your life
As three blind mice?

There was a crooked man

There was a crooked man,
And he walked a crooked mile,
He found a crooked sixpence
Upon a crooked stile;
He bought a crooked cat,
And it caught a crooked mouse,
And they all lived together
In a little crooked house.

I had a little nut tree

I had a little nut tree,
Nothing would it bear,
But a silver nutmeg
And a golden pear.
The King of Spain's daughter
Came to visit me,
And all for the sake
Of my little nut tree.

The north wind doth blow

The north wind doth blow,
And we shall have snow,
And what will the robin do then, poor thing?
He'll sit in a barn,
And keep himself warm,
And hide his head under his wing, poor thing!

Girls and boys, come out to play

Girls and boys, come out to play,
The moon doth shine as bright as day;
Leave your supper and leave your sleep,
And join your playfellows in the street.

Come with a whoop, and come with a call,
Come with a good will or come not at all;
Up the ladder and down the wall,
A penny loaf will serve us all.

Hey diddle, diddle

Hey diddle, diddle,
The cat and the fiddle,
The cow jumped over the moon;
The little dog laughed
To see such fun,
And the dish ran away with the spoon.

Jack and Jill

Jack and Jill went up the hill
To fetch a pail of water;
Jack fell down and broke his crown,
And Jill came tumbling after.

Up Jack got, and home did trot,
As fast as he could caper;
He went to bed to mend his head
With vinegar and brown paper.

Little Boy Blue

Little Boy Blue, come blow your horn,
The sheep's in the meadow, the cow's in the corn;
But where is the little boy who looks after the sheep?
He's under a haystack, fast asleep.
Will you go wake him? No, not I,
For if I do, he's sure to cry.

The Owl and the Pussy-cat

The Owl and the Pussy-cat went to sea
In a beautiful pea-green boat,
They took some honey, and plenty of money,
Wrapped up in a five-pound note.
The Owl looked up to the stars above,
And sang to a small guitar,
"O lovely Pussy! O Pussy, my love,
What a beautiful Pussy you are,
You are, you are!
What a beautiful Pussy you are!"

Pussy said to the Owl, "You elegant fowl,
How charmingly sweet you sing!
O let us be married! Too long we have tarried;
But what shall we do for a ring?"
They sailed away, for a year and a day,
To the land where the Bong-tree grows;
And there in a wood a Piggy-wig stood,
With a ring at the end of his nose,
His nose, his nose,
With a ring at the end of his nose.

turn the page

"Dear Pig, are you willing to sell for one shilling
Your ring?" Said the Piggy, "I will."
So they took it away, and were married next day
By the Turkey who lives on the hill.
They dined on mince, and slices of quince,
Which they ate with a runcible spoon;
And hand in hand, on the edge of the sand,
They danced by the light of the moon,
The moon, the moon,
They danced by the light of the moon.

Wee Willie Winkie

Wee Willie Winkie runs through the town,
Upstairs and downstairs in his nightgown,
Rapping at the window, crying through the lock,
Are the children all in bed,
for now it's eight o'clock?

The grand old Duke of York

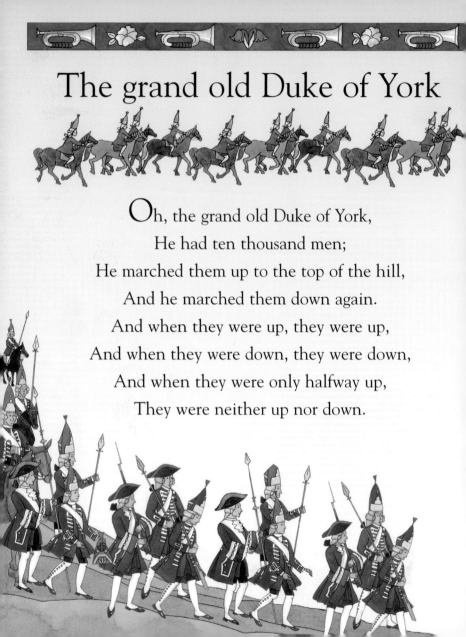

Oh, the grand old Duke of York,
He had ten thousand men;
He marched them up to the top of the hill,
And he marched them down again.
And when they were up, they were up,
And when they were down, they were down,
And when they were only halfway up,
They were neither up nor down.

Simple Simon

Simple Simon met a pieman
    Going to the fair;
Said Simple Simon to the pieman,
    "Let me taste your ware."

    Said the pieman unto Simon,
    "Show me first your penny;"
    Said Simple Simon to
      the pieman,
    "Sir, I haven't any."

Curly Locks

Curly Locks, Curly Locks,
Wilt thou be mine?
Thou shalt not wash dishes
Nor yet feed the swine,
But sit on a cushion
And sew a fine seam,
And feed upon strawberries,
Sugar and cream.

Two little dicky birds

Two little dicky birds,
Sitting on a wall;
One named Peter,
One named Paul.
Fly away, Peter!
Fly away, Paul!
Come back, Peter!
Come back, Paul!

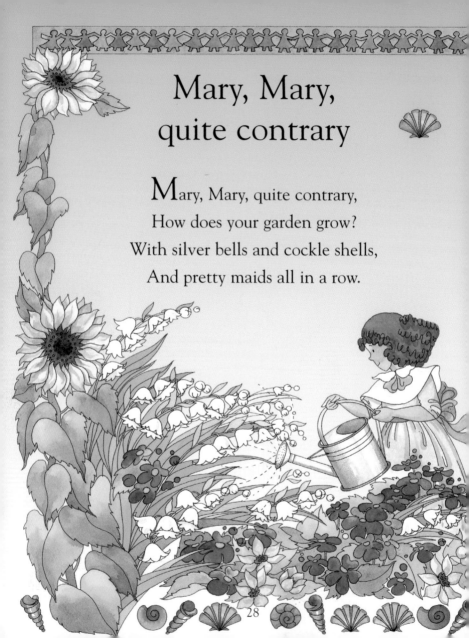

Mary, Mary,
quite contrary

Mary, Mary, quite contrary,
How does your garden grow?
With silver bells and cockle shells,
And pretty maids all in a row.

Itsy, bitsy spider

Itsy, bitsy spider
Climbed up the water spout;
Down came the rain
And washed the spider out.
Out came the sunshine
And dried up all the rain,
So the itsy, bitsy spider
Climbed up the spout again.

Twinkle, twinkle, little star

Twinkle, twinkle, little star,
How I wonder what you are,
Up above the world so high,
Like a diamond in the sky;
Twinkle, twinkle, little star,
How I wonder what you are.

Then the traveler in the dark
Thanks you for your tiny spark.
Could he see which way to go
If you did not twinkle so?
Twinkle, twinkle, little star,
How I wonder what you are.

In the dark blue sky you keep,
And often through my curtains peep;
For you never shut your eye
Till the sun is in the sky.
Twinkle, twinkle, little star,
How I wonder what you are.

Ring around the rosies

Ring around the rosies,
A pocket full of posies,
Ashes! Ashes!
We all fall down.

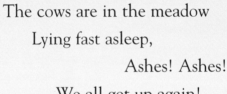

The cows are in the meadow
Lying fast asleep,
Ashes! Ashes!
We all get up again!

Ride a cock horse

Ride a cock horse to Banbury Cross,
To see a fine lady upon a white horse;
With rings on her fingers
And bells on her toes,
She shall have music wherever she goes.

Pussy-cat, Pussy-cat

Pussy-cat, Pussy-cat, where have you been?
I've been up to London to look at the Queen.
Pussy-cat, Pussy-cat, what did you there?
I frightened
a little mouse
under her chair.

Little Miss Muffet

Little Miss Muffet
Sat on a tuffet,
Eating her curds and whey;
Along came a spider,
Who sat down beside her,
And frightened
Miss Muffet
away!

Rock-a-bye, baby

Rock-a-bye, baby, on the tree-top,
When the wind blows, the cradle will rock;
When the bough breaks, the cradle will fall,

And down will come baby, cradle and all.

See-saw, Margery Daw

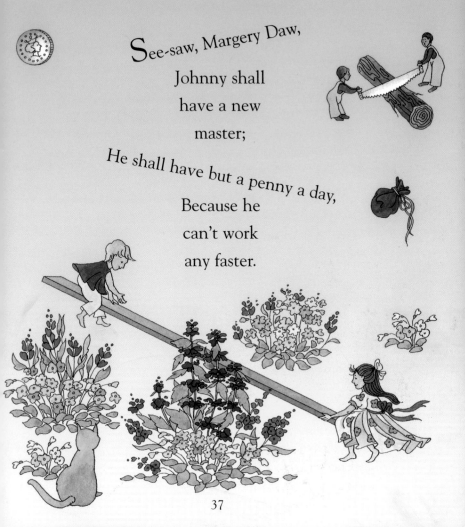

See-saw, Margery Daw,

Johnny shall
have a new
master;
He shall have but a penny a day,
Because he
can't work
any faster.

Old Mother Hubbard

Old Mother Hubbard
Went to the cupboard,
To fetch her poor dog a bone;
But when she got there
The cupboard was bare
And so the poor dog
had none.

Polly put the kettle on

Polly put the kettle on,
Polly put the kettle on,
Polly put the kettle on,
    We'll all have tea.

Sukey take it off again,
Sukey take it off again,
Sukey take it off again,
They've all gone away.

Lavender's blue

Lavender's blue, dilly, dilly,
Lavender's green,
When I am King, dilly, dilly,
You shall be Queen.

Call up your men, dilly, dilly,
Set them to work,
Some to the plow, dilly, dilly,
Some to the cart.

Some to make hay, dilly, dilly,
Some to make corn,
While you and I, dilly, dilly,
Keep ourselves warm.

Lavender's green, dilly, dilly,
Lavender's blue,
If you love me, dilly, dilly,
I will love you.

Goosey, goosey gander

Goosey, goosey gander,
whither would you wander?
Upstairs and downstairs
and in my lady's chamber.

There I met an old man
who wouldn't say his prayers;
So I took him by the left leg
and threw him down the stairs.

To market, to market

To market, to market to buy a fat pig,
Home again, home again, jiggetty-jig.

To market, to market to buy a fat hog,
Home again, home again, jiggetty-jog.

To market, to market to buy a plum bun,
Home again, home again, market is done.

I'm a little teapot

  I'm a little teapot, short and stout,
Here's my handle, here's my spout;
When I see a teacup, hear me shout,
"Lift me up,

and pour me out."

44

Little Tommy Tucker

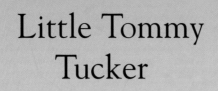

Little Tommy Tucker
   Sings for his supper.
      What shall we give him?
   White bread and butter.
How shall he cut it
Without e'er a knife?
   How shall he be married
      Without e'er a wife?

Pat-a-cake,
pat-a-cake

Pat-a-cake, pat-a-cake, baker's man,
Bake me a cake just as fast as you can;
Pat it and prick it, and mark it with B,
And put it in the oven for baby and me.

Lucy Locket

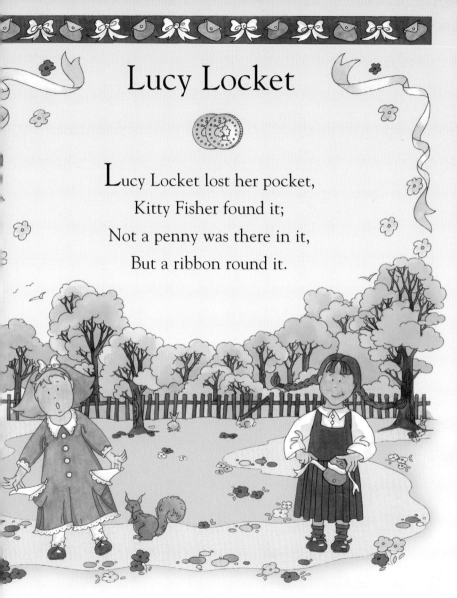

Lucy Locket lost her pocket,
Kitty Fisher found it;
Not a penny was there in it,
But a ribbon round it.

Hot cross buns

Hot cross buns!

Hot cross buns!

One a penny,

Two a penny,

Hot cross buns!

If you have no daughters,

Give them to your sons;

One a penny,

Two a penny,

Hot cross buns!

Pease pudding hot

Pease pudding hot,
Pease pudding cold,
Pease pudding in the pot,
Nine days old.
Some like it hot,
Some like it cold,
Some like it in the pot,
Nine days old.

Little Bo-Peep

Little Bo-Peep has lost her sheep,
And doesn't know where to find them;
Leave them alone, and they'll come home,
Wagging their tails behind them.

Little Bo-Peep fell fast asleep,
And dreamed that she heard them bleating
But when she awoke, she found it a joke,
For they were still a-fleeting.

Then up she took her little crook,
Determined for to find them;
She found them indeed, but it made her heart bleed,
For they'd left their tails behind them.

It happened one day, as Bo-Peep did stray
Into a meadow hard by;
That there she espied their tails side by side,
All hung on a tree to dry.

She heaved a sigh, and wiped her eye,
And over the hillocks went rambling,
And tried what she could, as a shepherdess should,
To tack each again to its lambkin.

Tom, Tom, the piper's son

Tom, Tom, the piper's son,
Stole a pig and away he run;
The pig was eat
And Tom was beat,
And Tom went howling down the street.

Hickory, dickory, dock

Hickory, dickory, dock!
The mouse ran up the clock;
The clock struck one,
The mouse ran down,
Hickory, dickory, dock!

There was
an old woman

There was an old woman
Who lived in a shoe,
She had so many children
She didn't know what to do;
She gave them some broth,
Without any bread,
Then whipped them all soundly
And sent them to bed.

Baa, baa, black sheep

Baa, baa, black sheep,
Have you any wool?
Yes sir, yes sir,
Three bags full:
One for the master,
And one for the dame,
And one for the little boy
Who lives down the lane.

One, two, three, four, five

One, two, three, four, five,
Once I caught a fish alive;
Six, seven, eight, nine, ten,
Then I let him go again.
Why did you let him go?
Because he bit my finger so.
Which finger did he bite?
This little finger on the right.

I love little kitty

I love little kitty,
Her coat is so warm,
And if I don't hurt her
She'll do me no harm.
So I'll not pull her tail,
Nor drive her away,
But kitty and I
Very gently will play.

Cock-a-doodle-doo

Cock-a-doodle-doo!
My dame has lost her shoe,
My master's lost his fiddling stick,
And doesn't know what to do.

Cock-a-doodle-doo!
My dame has found her shoe,
My master's found his fiddling stick,
So
Cock-a-doodle-doo!

58

Little Jack Horner

Little Jack Horner
Sat in a corner,
Eating his Christmas pie;
He put in his thumb,
And pulled out a plum,
And said "What a good boy am I!"

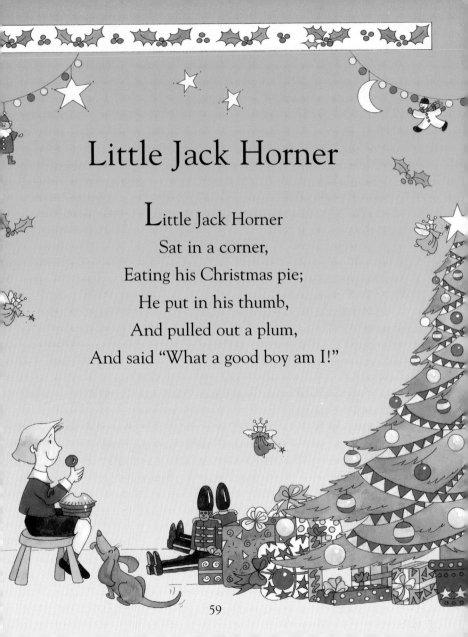

Pop goes the weasel

Half a pound of tuppenny rice,
Half a pound of treacle,
Mix it up and make it nice,
Pop goes the weasel!

Up and down the city road,
In and out the eagle,
That's the way the money goes,
Pop goes the weasel!

Every night when I go out,
The monkey's on the table,
Take a stick and knock it off,
Pop goes the weasel!

A penny for a spool of thread,
A penny for a needle,
That's the way the money goes,
Pop goes the weasel!

All around the cobbler's bench,
The monkey chased the people;
The donkey thought 'twas all in fun,
Pop goes the weasel!

Games and actions

Some of the nursery rhymes in this book have actions or games to go with them. You can read about these over the next few pages.

Humpty Dumpty

⋆ Sit down on the floor with your knees against your chest and wrap your arms around your knees.
⋆ Rock gently backward and forward as you say the rhyme.
⋆ When you reach the line "Humpty Dumpty had a great fall," roll over backward.
⋆ Keep reciting, and without letting go of your knees, try to sit up again. (This is harder than it sounds!)
⋆ The player who does this first wins.

The grand old Duke of York

⋆ Start marching on the spot.
⋆ March forward when you say "up."
⋆ March backward when you say "down."
⋆ Take one step forward, then one step back, when you say "neither up nor down."

Two little dicky birds

⋆ Stick a stamp on the end of each index finger.
⋆ Wiggle one finger when you say "Peter" and wiggle the other for "Paul."
⋆ On "Fly away, Peter" put the finger called Peter behind your back, and hide the other finger when you say "Fly away, Paul."
⋆ Bring Peter and then Paul out from behind your back when you say "Come back, Peter! Come back, Paul!"

Itsy, bitsy spider

* As you say "Itsy, bitsy spider climbed up the water spout," touch each index finger with the opposite thumb.
* Make a climbing action by twisting them opposite ways until they touch again.
* When you say "Down came the rain" wiggle your fingers like raindrops and bring your hands down.
* For "Out came the sunshine," put your hands in an arch over your head.
* Repeat the climbing action for the last part of the rhyme.

I'm a little teapot

* When you say "Here's my handle," put one hand on your hip.
* When you say "Here's my spout," put your other arm out to the side like the spout of a teapot.
* During the last line, lean sideways as if you are pouring the tea.

Pat-a-cake, pat-a-cake

* Clap your hands while you say the first line, and rub them together in the second line.
* Next, pretend to prick one of your hands with the first finger of the other.
* Then, as you say the last line, pretend you are putting a cake into the oven.

Ring around the rosies

* While you say this rhyme, all hold hands and step around in a circle.
* When you say "We all fall down," crouch down as low as you can.
* Then, as you say "We all get up again," jump up as high as you can.

Pease pudding hot

This rhyme can be used as a clapping game. To play, you have to stand facing a partner. There are four different clapping movements:
⋆ Clap both hands against your partner's hands.
⋆ Clap your own hands together.
⋆ Clap your right hand against your partner's right hand.
⋆ Clap your left hand against your partner's left hand.
Repeat this, saying the lines faster and faster, until one of you makes a mistake.

One, two, three, four, five

⋆ Count up to five by holding up your fingers.
⋆ When you say "Once I caught a fish alive," pretend to catch a fish that is wiggling around in your hands.
⋆ Count six to ten on your fingers.
⋆ Then, pretend to throw the fish back into the water.
⋆ Shake your hand on "bit my finger."
⋆ Hold up the little finger on your right hand when you say "This little finger on the right."

Hickory, dickory dock

You can use this rhyme to decide who starts a game. As you say the words, point at each player in turn. When you reach the end of the rhyme, the person that you are pointing at starts the game.

Additional design by Katie Mayes • Digital manipulation by Nick Wakeford
This edition adapted by Leonie Pratt • Americanization by Carrie Armstrong
This edition first published in 2005 by Usborne Publishing Ltd, Usborne House, 83-85 Saffron Hill, London EC1N 8RT, England.
www.usborne.com Copyright © 2005, 2003, 1996 Usborne Publishing Ltd. The name Usborne and the devices ♀ ☺ are Trade
Marks of Usborne Publishing Ltd. All rights reserved. No part of this publication may be reproduced, stored in a retrieval system or
transmitted in any form or by any means, electronic, mechanical, photocopying, recording or otherwise, without the prior permission
of the publisher. Printed in China. AE. First published in America in 2005.